The Boxcar Children® Mysteries

THE HURRICANE MYSTERY

created by
GERTRUDE CHANDLER WARNER

Illustrated by Charles Tang

ALBERT WHITMAN & Company
Morton Grove, Illinois

Library of Congress Cataloging-in-Publication Data
is available from the Library of Congress.

The Hurricane Mystery (#54 in The Boxcar Children Series)
ISBN 0-8075-3436-6 (hardcover)
ISBN 0-8075-3437-4 (paperback)

Cover art by David Cunningham

Contents

THE HURRICANE MYSTERY

CHAPTER 1

Hurricanes and Pirates

"Do you think we'll see any pirates?" asked Benny Alden. He pressed his face against the window of the taxi and peered out at the drawbridge that was raised in front of them.

"Oh, Benny!" said his sister Jessie. She was twelve, six years older than Benny. "Of course not. No pirates live in Charleston!"

"Where do they live?" asked Benny. A fishing boat, hung with nets, slid through the narrow channel of marshy water beneath the bridge. The drawbridge began to close.

"Pirates lived a long, long time ago, Benny," said fourteen-year-old Henry Alden. "There are no pirates now."

Benny looked disappointed. He said stubbornly, "I'm going to be a pirate when I grow up anyway. I'll have a big ship, and Watch and I will make people walk the plank!"

The other Aldens laughed at that. Watch Alden, a small black and white terrier curled on Henry's lap, barked.

Then ten-year-old Violet, always gentle and kind, said, "Benny, you wouldn't make anybody really walk the plank. Would you?"

"Maybe not," said Benny. "I guess I can't be a real pirate after all. But I still wish I could see one."

Suddenly the taxi driver spoke. "And even if you don't see any pirates, young man, you might see a pirate's treasure."

Benny bounced up and down in excitement. "Really?"

"You never know," said the cab driver. "After all, the legends and stories all say that pirates used to stop on Sullivans Island. The famous writer Edgar Allan Poe even wrote a story about finding pirate gold buried there! The library on Sullivans Island is named after him: the Edgar Allan Poe Library."

After the drawbridge closed, they crossed the bridge to Sullivans Island, a small island off the coast of Charleston, South Carolina. The Alden children and their grandfather were on their way to visit Mrs. Ellen Ashleigh, who lived in one of the big old houses on the island. A hurricane had recently blown through Charleston, and right across Sullivans Island. Benny forgot about pirates when he saw what the hurricane had done.

"How fast does the wind from a hurricane blow?" asked Benny, staring at a house that had no roof at all.

"Hurricanes are the strongest of all the storms," answered Grandfather Alden. "The winds can blow a hundred and fifty miles an hour or more."

"It blew the water from the ocean right across this island," said the cab driver. "It filled all the houses with water and mud."

"Look at that boat!" exclaimed Jessie. The hurricane had left a boat behind on the middle of the island, right in the center of the road.

"Yep," said the cab driver, carefully driving his car around the boat. "This was one of the worst hurricanes yet. It blew whole houses away. Cars and boats, too. But we'll rebuild. We've never let a hurricane defeat us yet!"

He pulled the cab to a stop in front of a large two-story silvery gray house with a wide front porch. Instead of corners at each end, it had round rooms on both the first and second floor, like towers.

Shutters framed the windows. Some of them were closed, with boards nailed across them. Railings were missing from the porch. A tree had fallen in the yard. Boards had been ripped from the porch itself. And there were no front steps! But someone had already been cleaning up. A pile of branches was heaped neatly in one side of the yard.

"Oh, dear," said Violet. "Did the hurricane do all that?"

"Don't worry, Violet. We can fix it," said Henry confidently.

"Yes," agreed Jessie. "After all, that's why we're here — to help Mrs. Ashleigh fix her house."

"Good luck," said the cab driver as the Aldens got out of the cab. He winked at Benny. "And good luck finding that pirate's treasure!" he added.

Just then a tall, graceful woman with short black and silver hair came hurrying out of the house. She stepped carefully off the front porch and held out her hands as she walked up to them. "James Alden," she said. "I'm so glad to see you. I'm so glad to see all of you!"

She hugged Mr. Alden and all of the Aldens, even Watch. Then she led the way back to the house. "Watch your step," she said when they reached the front porch.

"The hurricane blew our front steps away. I imagine they are at the bottom of the ocean now!"

Suddenly Benny started to laugh. "It's just like the step for our boxcar," he said. He pointed. Where the front steps had been, Mrs. Ashleigh had put a stump as a temporary step.

"Your boxcar?" asked Mrs. Ashleigh.

"We used to live in a boxcar," said Jessie. "Before Grandfather found us."

The Boxcar Children told Mrs. Ashleigh about how, after their parents had died, they had gone to live in an old boxcar in the woods. They didn't know that their grandfather was looking for them and wanted them to come live with him. When he found them, he'd brought them all to his house in Greenfield. As a surprise, and to make them feel more at home, he'd brought the boxcar, too. He'd put it behind the house and now they could visit it whenever they wanted.

Hearing the story of the Boxcar Children,

Mrs. Ashleigh smiled. "Well, I'm glad my house has a stump for a front step, just like your boxcar does, then," she said. "It will make you feel more at home."

"But soon you'll have stairs," said Henry. "Because we'll fix them for you."

Watch gave a little bark and hopped up the stump onto the front porch. He looked over his shoulder at everyone as if to say, *Let's get to work.*

"Okay, boy. Here we come," said Benny. And the Aldens went inside with Mrs. Ashleigh.

Inside the house Jessie said, "But there is no furniture! Oh, dear, Mrs. Ashleigh! Did the hurricane blow it all away?"

Mrs. Ashleigh laughed and shook her head. "No. With the help of my neighbors, I got the furniture moved upstairs before the hurricane hit. Now that things are drying out and I've got most of the first floor cleaned up and repainted, I've just started moving it back down. We boarded up the windows and the water didn't get any higher than the first floor. I was one of the lucky people. I didn't lose much. Except . . ." She stopped and sighed.

"What?" said Violet, clasping her hands.

"Well, the hurricane took one very, very valuable thing of mine," said Mrs. Ashleigh. "The most valuable thing I own. It's priceless. The Pirate's Gate."

CHAPTER 2

Lost and Found

Benny's eyes grew very round. "The Pirate's Gate?" he cried. "See? I told you there were pirates!"

He gave a little skip of excitement. Grandfather put his hand on Benny's shoulder. "Slow down, Benny. Let's hear the rest of the story."

"But first why don't y'all get unpacked and settled in your rooms," suggested Mrs. Ashleigh. "I'll be in the kitchen and when you are ready, we can have some refreshments and I'll tell you about the Pirate's Gate."

"Hurry!" Benny said. Then he added, "I'm hungry!" Watch barked in agreement.

Mrs. Ashleigh showed the Aldens where to go. Then she went back to the kitchen.

Each of the Aldens had a separate room upstairs in the big house. As they all hurried to unpack, they discovered that Mrs. Ashleigh had put the downstairs furniture in every single room upstairs. Violet found boxes of books and china, and four rugs rolled up in her room. Henry had five chairs, a coffee table, and a giant hanging fern crammed into his. Benny laughed and laughed when he saw that his room was filled with lamps — tall and short, fat and skinny, fancy and plain. Jessie's room had tables and pillows and pictures in picture frames propped against the wall. Even the halls were lined with furniture and boxes that Mrs. Ashleigh had put upstairs to keep safe from the storm, in case the ocean came into the house.

"The hurricane made waves as tall as a

house," Violet said in an awed voice.

"Yes," said Grandfather Alden, his face serious. "The wind can blow your house away. Or the waves can wash it away. Ellen was lucky her house withstood the hurricane. Some people weren't so lucky."

"We'll have to help Mrs. Ashleigh move the rest of her furniture back downstairs," said Henry, as the four of them and Watch made their way back downstairs to the kitchen.

"Yes," agreed Jessie. "That will be one of our first jobs."

In the kitchen, they were glad to see that Mrs. Ashleigh had already moved the table and chairs back downstairs. They sat around the table, and Mrs. Ashleigh served them lemonade and cookies. She gave Watch a bowl of fresh water and Benny gave him a dog biscuit.

Mrs. Ashleigh looked at Watch. "You're a very good dog, aren't you, Watch?"

Watch wagged his tail.

"Smart, too," put in Jessie. She was about

to tell Mrs. Ashleigh how Watch had helped solve mysteries, and had even mysteriously disappeared himself once.

But Benny couldn't wait any longer.

"Tell us about the Pirate's Gate!" Benny burst out. "Do pirates use it?"

Mrs. Ashleigh shook her head and smiled a little sadly. "No. But a pirate may have built it, Benny."

"Who?" asked Benny excitedly.

"My great-great-great-great-grandfather," said Mrs. Ashleigh. "His name was Fitzhugh, Forrest Fitzhugh. He came to Charleston when it was a little town at the end of the harbor. No one knew where he came from or how he got so much money, but he was a very wealthy man. He met my great-great-great-great-grandmother, Ellen, and fell in love. They got married and settled in Charleston. As a wedding present he gave her a beautiful house in Charleston, the house where I grew up and where my son lives now. She loved to garden so he designed a special gate for her garden."

"Oh, that's *so* romantic," said Violet, her eyes shining.

"Why is it called the Pirate's Gate?" asked Jessie.

"What did the gate look like?" asked Henry.

Mrs. Ashleigh held up her hand and laughed. "One at a time, okay? It was called the Pirate's Gate for two reasons. One, many people believed that Mr. Fitzhugh had made his fortune as a pirate before he met Ellen and settled down. So they said when you went to visit Mr. Fitzhugh, you went in by a pirate's gate. When Mr. Fitzhugh found out about it, he named his house — the house I grew up in, over in Charleston — Pirate's Gate."

"People also said he kept it hidden nearby." She paused and smiled. "When I was a little girl, I used to dig all over that backyard in Charleston, looking for buried treasure."

"What's the other reason it was called the Pirate's Gate?" asked Benny impatiently.

"Well, the gate was made of black wrought iron. It was taller than your brother Henry and it had a ship set right in the middle of it."

"A pirate's ship!" cried Benny.

"Maybe, Benny. But no one's ever been able to prove it, and Mr. Fitzhugh never said. He never denied he was a pirate, though. He just laughed and said there was nothing he couldn't do. They say that was true, too. He *could* do anything — mend a sail or shoe a horse.

"Anyway, I brought the gate with me when I moved from Charleston to Sullivans Island after my husband died. This house was our family's summer house. Our family has spent summer vacations here since before I was born."

"And now the gate is gone," said Violet sadly. She pushed her glass of lemonade away.

"If only I'd had those old hinges fixed, it might still be here," said Mrs. Ashleigh. "Maybe it would have been strong enough to outlast the wind and waves of the hurricane."

"Maybe it hasn't gone far," said Henry. He jumped up. "We could go look for it."

"That's very nice of you, Henry, but I expect that gate is at the bottom of the ocean," said Mrs. Ashleigh. "Along with my front steps!"

"It might not be," said Violet. "And we are good at finding things and solving mysteries. Aren't we, Grandfather?"

"That's true," said Mr. Alden.

"Well, it can't hurt to look," said Mrs. Ashleigh. "And you'll get a chance to explore the island. It's a small island. You can't get lost, and everybody is very friendly."

The Aldens thanked Mrs. Ashleigh for their lemonade and cookies. Then they hurried out of the house to begin to search for the Pirate's Gate.

Blue skies arched overhead. The sun shone bright and clear and warm. Everywhere they looked, they saw people cleaning up the mess the hurricane left behind. Some people carried trees and branches and debris to big piles at the edge of the street. Others hammered and sawed and nailed, taking the boards off windows and replacing broken glass. People waved at the children as they walked by.

Seeing all the things the hurricane had blown away, Jessie shook her head. "I'm afraid Mrs. Ashleigh is right. That gate could be at the bottom of the ocean by now."

"Oh, no, it's not," said Benny. He pointed. "Look," he said. "There it is!"

Two women were dragging a gate across the front yard of a house that looked newer and fancier than many of the other houses they'd seen on the island. The gate they were dragging was big and made of iron shaped into bars and scrolls. And it had a ship made of iron set right in the middle of it!

"Careful!" they heard the shorter of the two women say. She was thin and had short black hair that curled around her pale face. She struggled with the heavy gate. Her khaki pants and ivory-colored sandals were spattered with mud, but she didn't seem to care.

"We don't want to damage this any more than the hurricane has!"

"Don't worry, Jackie, I won't drop it," panted the taller of the two women. She was wearing jeans and work boots that were also muddy. Her brown hair was pulled back into a ponytail with a bandanna. She had freckles sprinkled across her sunburned nose.

"When I say go, lift the gate into the back of my van," said the first woman. "Ready, set, go!"

The two women lifted the gate in the air and set it down gently on an old blanket. The shorter woman closed the van. "Thanks, Diana," she said. "I appreciate your help." She took keys from her pocket and walked quickly toward the driver's side.

The Aldens exchanged glances. What was this woman going to do with Mrs. Ashleigh's gate?

"Stop!" shouted Henry. "That's the Pirate's Gate. It doesn't belong to you!"

CHAPTER 3

A Paper Chase

The shorter woman spun around and dropped her car keys.

The taller woman put her hands on her hips. "Who are you?" she demanded.

"I'm Henry Alden. These are my sisters, Jessie and Violet, my brother, Benny, and our dog, Watch." He pointed. "And that is Mrs. Ashleigh's gate."

"How do you know that?" asked the shorter woman.

Now Jessie put her hands on her own hips. "Mrs. Ashleigh told us," she said.

The shorter woman, who'd bent over to pick up her car keys, straightened up. Red spots of color flushed her pale cheeks. "For that matter, how do you know Mrs. Ashleigh?" she asked.

"Our grandfather is a friend of hers," said Jessie. "We came all the way from Greenfield to help her clean and fix up her house. She told us about the hurricane blowing her gate away."

The taller woman suddenly laughed. "You know, I thought that gate looked familiar, didn't you, Jackie?" To the Aldens, she said, "The hurricane dropped it in Jackie's backyard. I was helping her put it in the truck."

"To take to Ellen Ashleigh," said Jackie. "I told you that, didn't I, Diana?"

"Did you?" Diana scratched her head. "I've had so much carpenter work to do lately, since the hurricane, that I feel as if I have a hurricane blowing my thoughts around." She stuck out her hand. "Hi. I'm Diana Shelby. I'm a neighbor of Mrs. Ashleigh's."

"Me, too," said Jackie. "I'm Jacqueline James. Everybody calls me Jackie. Sorry if I was a little suspicious. But after a hurricane, all kinds of characters arrive to try to take advantage of people. I guess we'd better hurry and get this gate back to Ellen."

"Do you need me to help you take it out of the van?" asked Diana.

"We'll help," volunteered Henry.

"Fine," said Diana. "I'd better be getting to my next job. A man at the other end of the island had all the doors blown off his house. I've got to put some new ones up for him." Diana walked over to a battered pickup truck and got in and drove quickly away.

"Why don't I give y'all a ride back to Mrs. Ashleigh's?" suggested Jackie.

The Aldens thought this was a very good idea.

"I'll go the long way around," Jackie said. "That way, you can see some more of the island." She drove them down the quiet streets, waving at people as she passed. "Out there is the lighthouse," she said. She pointed. "And over there is the library."

"The Edgar Allan Poe library," said Jessie.

"Yes!" answered Jackie, looking surprised that Jessie knew that.

"We solved a mystery in a library once," said Henry.

"A *deserted* library," added Benny. In a few minutes they'd reached Mrs. Ashleigh's house. Benny bounced out of the van and ran toward the house shouting, "Mrs. Ashleigh, Mrs. Ashleigh! Come here quickly! We've found your gate."

The door opened and Mrs. Ashleigh and Grandfather Alden hurried out. Grandfather was still holding his glass of lemonade.

"Ellen!" cried Jackie, climbing out of the van. She walked around to the back of the van and opened it. With a sweep of her arm she said, "Look what the hurricane left in my backyard!"

Mrs. Ashleigh's eyes widened. She put

one hand up to her mouth and walked slowly forward. "It can't be," she said. "I don't believe it!"

"It is," said Jessie. "See, I told you we were good at finding things."

Violet said, "We've only been here for a few hours, and we've already solved a mystery!"

"You certainly have, Violet. The Pirate's Gate," said Mrs. Ashleigh. "I never thought I'd see it again."

"The Aldens found me loading it into my van to bring back to you," Jackie explained. "Naturally I recognized it right away. I was very careful with it, but I'm afraid the hurricane did some damage."

"That can be fixed," said Mrs. Ashleigh, patting the gate as if it were alive. "Oh, I'm so glad to see it again."

With the help of the Aldens, Jackie lifted the gate out of the van and carried it to the edge of the house. She propped it against the front porch.

"Won't you come in and have some lemonade?" Mrs. Ashleigh asked Jackie. But Jackie shook her head and smiled. "I have to go. I have a business to run — we're not as busy as we should be, but there are a few tourists who still come to Charleston looking for a carriage ride!" She turned to the Aldens and said, "When you get a chance, come into town. I'll give you a tour in an old-fashioned horse and carriage, compliments of Hoofbeats of History. That's the name of my guide business."

"Horses?" said Benny. "I'd like that."

Mrs. Ashleigh said, "Thank you again, Jackie. Now I'm going to go call William Farrier. He's done ironwork for me before."

"Of course! He's the very man to fix your gate," said Jackie. She said good-bye and left.

"Wow," said Jessie as the Aldens went back into the house with Mrs. Ashleigh and Grandfather. "Wouldn't that be fun, to drive a horse and carriage and give tours to people?"

"I'd like that," agreed Henry.

"Me, too," said Benny. "Second, after being a pirate."

"Who's William Farrier?" asked Violet.

"I think you all would like his job, too," said Mrs. Ashleigh. "He started out as a blacksmith, but now he's a famous craftsman and artist. He works in wrought and cast iron. When you go to Charleston you'll see lots of lovely iron gates and balconies and fences. Some are as old as the Pirate's Gate and some are new, designed and made by people like Mr. Farrier."

While they were waiting for Mr. Farrier to arrive, the Aldens helped Mrs. Ashleigh take some of the furniture that had been moved upstairs, back downstairs into the rooms that had been cleaned out and re-painted. Since they were the biggest and strongest, Grandfather and Henry moved the biggest pieces of furniture: a desk, some bookshelves, and some tables. Violet and Benny carried lamps down. Jessie and Mrs. Ashleigh unrolled the rugs on the floors.

Jessie had just begun to help Mrs. Ashleigh bring down boxes of books for the study shelves when someone knocked on the front door.

A short, strong-looking man with power-ful hands and a small pair of gold wire-rim glasses perched on the end of his nose stood there. He was wearing jeans and a plaid flan-nel shirt with the sleeves rolled up. He was carrying a toolbox.

"Mr. Farrier! I'm so glad you could come," said Mrs. Ashleigh.

"I've met the Pirate's Gate before," said Mr. Farrier, his brown eyes twinkling be-hind his glasses. He nodded toward where the gate was propped against the house. "I look forward to a chance to work on it."

Mrs. Ashleigh and the Aldens followed Mr. Farrier as he went to look at the gate. "Can it be fixed?" Mrs. Ashleigh asked anxiously.

"I don't believe the hurricane did any dam-age that I can't put right," said Mr. Farrier. "But it's a very old gate, so I can't say for

sure. I'd like to take it back to my shop to work on it there."

"Of course," said Mrs. Ashleigh.

"I'll just do a little work on these hinges first," said Mr. Farrier. "They didn't get too banged up. I'll be finished in no time."

After Mr. Farrier had fixed the hinges on the iron fence where the gate had hung, the Aldens once again helped carry the gate across the front yard, this time to load onto Mr. Farrier's red truck. "I'll let you know in a day or two about the gate," said Mr. Farrier.

"Thank you," said Mrs. Ashleigh.

"Can we come watch you shoe horses?" asked Benny.

"Well, I don't shoe horses much anymore," said Mr. Farrier with a slow smile. "But you can visit me at my shop, Farrier's Studio. It's right down in Charleston. Anybody can tell you where it is."

"Oh, good," said Jessie. "Thank you."

The Aldens went back to work. All the rest of the day they moved furniture, shelved books, and helped Mrs. Ashleigh clean up around the house. By dinnertime, all the books were back on the study shelves, and when Jessie turned on the desk lamp, the room had a cozy glow.

"It is exactly the way it was before the hurricane," said Mrs. Ashleigh, looking pleased.

Just then Henry staggered through the door with a huge box in his arms. "There are five more of these upstairs," he said.

"Woof!" said Watch, jumping up to say hello to Henry.

"Look out!" cried Jessie. But it was too late. Henry lost his balance and dropped the box.

Violet covered her ears.

Watch scampered quickly out of the way.

The top of the box came off. Files spilled out and paper flew everywhere!

CHAPTER 4

A Terrible Fight

"Uh-oh!" said Henry.

"We'll help you clean it up," said Violet.

"Don't worry," said Mrs. Ashleigh. She walked quickly to the overturned box. "But be careful! Some of these papers are very, very old."

Benny knelt down by the box. "Look," he said. "A picture!"

"That's Mr. Fitzhugh," said Mrs. Ashleigh.

"The pirate!" Benny gasped, his eyes round.

"Maybe so," Mrs. Ashleigh answered. "We can just put the papers back in the box. I have to go through them anyway."

"Look at this," said Jessie.

"Is it a pirate's map for treasure?" asked Benny excitedly.

Jessie laughed. "No, Benny. But it is a drawing of something."

"The original plans for the house that Mr. Fitzhugh built in Charleston. And here are the original plans for the Pirate's Gate. They all go in this envelope," said Mrs. Ashleigh.

"These should be in a safe place," said Henry.

Mrs. Ashleigh nodded. "I know. I'm going to go through them and give them to the local museum."

"Does the museum have dinosaurs in it?" asked Benny. He was thinking about another mystery the Aldens had solved.

"No, Benny, it's not that kind of museum," said Mrs. Ashleigh. "It's a museum about Charleston."

"We can help you go through the papers, too," said Jessie. "It will be fun."

"We'll start right away!" agreed Henry.

Mrs. Ashleigh held up her hand. "Tomorrow is soon enough. Right now, I think it's time for dinner."

"Good," said Benny. "We've worked hard today. We even solved a mystery. That always makes me hungry!"

In the next few days, the sounds of hammers and saws could be heard all over the island as people repaired their houses. The Boxcar Children worked hard helping Mrs. Ashleigh. Soon they'd finished moving furniture and were nailing new floorboards on the porch. They put fresh paint on all the window frames and shutters. When the porch was ready, they planned to paint that, too. They also ran errands and, in the late afternoons, explored the island and played on the wide, smooth beaches.

One day, on their way to the small island grocery store to pick up milk for Mrs. Ashleigh, they saw Diana working on a house. She waved them over.

"How's everything going?" Diana asked. She reknotted the rubber band she had around her ponytail and smoothed her hair back.

The Aldens told her what they'd been doing and asked Diana questions about her work. She told them a couple of stories about the island and asked them questions about Mrs. Ashleigh and her house.

"That house of hers is one of the oldest on the island," said Diana. "It's been here since the 1800s and has survived lots and lots of hurricanes. They just don't build them like they used to!"

"We saw the plans for Mrs. Ashleigh's house in Charleston," Henry said. "They're in the old papers that we're helping her sort out."

"Really?" said Diana. "Well, well, well. Soon you'll be looking for old Mr. Fitzhugh's pirate treasure, too, won't you?"

"How did you know about that?" cried Benny.

"Oh, everybody knows about that story," said Diana. "It's a good one. Part of Charleston history."

"You don't believe there's really any treasure?" asked Jessie.

"Nah. And I wouldn't waste my time looking for make-believe treasure," said Diana. "I've got too much work to do. Time is money and I need all the money I can get."

She shook her head. "A hurricane is a bad thing, but it's meant a lot of work for me. But then, I guess you could say disaster repair is my specialty. Hurricanes, earthquakes — "

"Earthquakes, too?" asked Benny.

"Well, I lived in San Francisco for a while, near the Golden Gate Bridge. San Francisco has lots of earthquakes. I helped people earthquake-proof their houses. But Charleston's had earthquakes, too."

Diana picked up her hammer.

"Well, we won't keep you from your work," said Henry politely.

"See you later," said Diana. "Happy treasure hunting." She laughed.

"Everybody knows about Mr. Fitzhugh's treasure," said Benny, discouraged, as they walked away. "If they haven't found it, how can we?"

"It sounds as if most people don't even believe there is a treasure," said Violet.

"It sounds to me as if she was trying to discourage us from looking for the treasure," said Jessie. "Like she doesn't want us to believe there is one."

"So she can look for it herself?" Henry asked. "Hmmm. Maybe so."

"Because we could solve the mystery and find the treasure first," said Benny. "I'd like that."

"We all would," said Henry.

"Let's go look at those papers right now!" Benny urged.

"We have to stop at the grocery store first, Benny," Violet reminded him.

"I'll wait here with Watch," said Benny.

Henry, Jessie, and Violet went into the store to buy milk. Suddenly Henry said, "I have an idea. Let's make a pretend map and put it on top of the papers. We can let Benny find it and we can go on a treasure hunt tomorrow afternoon when we finish working."

"Oh, Benny will like that," said Jessie. She pointed and laughed. "And I have an idea for the treasure we can bury!"

"Do you want me to carry the milk for you?" Benny asked Violet when they came out of the store. But Violet shook her head and kept a firm hold on the grocery bag.

"Thanks, but I'll carry it, Benny," she said.

"Come on, then!" said Benny. He and Watch raced ahead and his brother and sisters hurried to catch up.

When they had put the groceries away, the children hurried to the study. The door was closed. And when Henry reached out to turn the knob, they heard the sound of an angry voice coming from inside.

"Why won't you listen to me?" a man almost shouted.

"Because it's my house, not yours!" said another quieter voice, fiercely.

"That's Mrs. Ashleigh!" gasped Violet.

"Well, it won't be yours for long," said the man. "You'd better sell before something worse happens to it. And to you!"

The door to the study slammed open and a tall man stormed out. He didn't even seem to see the Aldens standing in the hall. "Stubborn," he muttered under his breath. "She'll be sorry!" He stomped to the front door, slamming it on his way out.

Jessie rushed into the study with the others behind her. Mrs. Ashleigh had slumped into a chair by the window. She was staring out, her hands on her cheeks.

"Mrs. Ashleigh," said Jessie, trying to sound calm. "Are you all right?"

Mrs. Ashleigh looked up slowly. She blinked, as if surprised to see everyone. Then she shook her head. "I'm fine, dear. It's just that . . ." Her voice trailed off and she sighed.

"Who was that? Why was he threatening you?" said Henry. "We could hear him all the way out in the hall."

Mrs. Ashleigh didn't seem to hear Henry. She turned to stare out the window again. "It's my house," she said. "I'm not going to sell it. No matter what happens. And he can't make me. No matter how much money anyone offers me. This is my *home*."

"Who's trying to make you sell your house?" asked Jessie.

"Who was that mean man?" asked Benny.

Mrs. Ashleigh turned back to look at them. A sad smile crossed her face. "That mean man," she said, "was my son, Forrest Ashleigh."

CHAPTER 5

Hoofbeats of History

"Your son!" exclaimed Henry. He was very surprised.

"But . . ." Jessie began, then stopped. It would be rude to say what the Boxcar Children were all thinking: that Mrs. Ashleigh was so nice, but her son didn't seem nice at all.

"I'm sorry I called your son a mean man," said Benny contritely.

Mrs. Ashleigh shook her head sadly.

"That's all right, Benny. You didn't know he was my son."

"Why does he want you to sell your house?" asked Violet softly.

"He's just worried about me. He says it's not safe. Hurricanes hit this island often, you know. This last one wasn't the first, nor the worst. And another hurricane could come along at any time," said Mrs. Ashleigh.

"But this house has been here for years and years without a hurricane blowing it away," said Henry. "Diana Shelby told us that. She said the old houses are the strongest."

"I wish she could meet Forrest and convince him of that." Mrs. Ashleigh took a deep breath and stood up. "But let's not think about that now." She smiled at the four children. "I have some good news for you. You're fired."

"Fired?" said Jessie. "But why? What did we do wrong?"

"Uh-oh," said Benny.

Mrs. Ashleigh smiled. This time it wasn't

a sad smile. "You didn't do anything wrong. You're only fired for tomorrow. We all need a break from work. I'm declaring tomorrow a holiday!"

"And tonight we're going out to dinner," said Grandfather Alden, walking into the room. "Right here on the island. Ellen's favorite restaurant, the Crab House, has just reopened."

Mrs. Ashleigh looked a little more cheerful. "I'm so glad," she said. "What a wonderful idea, James. We've all been working too hard!"

Everyone hurried to get ready to go out to dinner. Then they went downstairs and waited on the big front porch while Benny went to the kitchen to fill Watch's water bowl with fresh water and give Watch his own dinner.

"Be a good dog and watch the house," Benny told Watch. "Maybe I'll bring you some leftovers." He paused and added thoughtfully, "If there are any!"

Like everything on the small island, the

restaurant wasn't far away. The Aldens and Mrs. Ashleigh strolled down the quiet streets.

"I've been at home working so hard on my house, I haven't seen how much work everyone else has done on theirs," admitted Mrs. Ashleigh.

In the restaurant, Mrs. Ashleigh seemed to know almost everyone. The Aldens met lots of new people.

And they saw one familiar face.

"Look! There's Jackie," said Benny. He waved.

Jackie got up from her table and came over to say hello. "A big crowd tonight," she said, motioning to all the people in the restaurant. "The hurricane doesn't seem to have hurt the Crab House's business."

"Everyone's been working hard," said Mrs. Ashleigh. "They're probably glad to take a break, just like we are."

"Tomorrow we have a holiday," added Jessie. "We're not going to work at all."

Jackie smiled. "You've been a lot of help to Ellen, haven't you?"

"Oh, yes," said Benny. "We have moved furniture and cleaned and we're even helping go through lots of old papers. Pirate papers."

Raising one eyebrow, Jackie looked at Mrs. Ashleigh. "Some of those papers are very old and fragile," she said.

"The Aldens are being careful," Mrs. Ashleigh said. "We'll have them ready for the museum in no time."

Jackie looked as if she didn't quite believe Mrs. Ashleigh. "Let me know if you need help," she said. Then, as if sorry for sounding a little rude, she said, "If tomorrow is a holiday, why don't you come to town? Drive into Charleston and take a carriage tour with Hoofbeats of History, just like I promised you?"

"That would be fun!" said Violet.

"I think it's a grand idea," said Mrs. Ashleigh.

"Good," said Jackie. "Be there at ten tomorrow! You can even bring your dog. Have a good dinner."

"We will," said Mrs. Ashleigh. "How do lobsters and crab cakes sound, Benny?"

"Crab cakes? Can I have *chocolate* cake instead?" asked Benny. Everybody laughed.

Early the next morning, Henry sneaked down and put a special "pirate's map" on top of a pile of carefully sorted papers in the study. Jessie and Violet hurried out to bury the "treasure" for Benny to find later that day.

Then, right after breakfast, all the Aldens and Mrs. Ashleigh drove to Charleston. They passed Diana working on a house just down the street and waved as they went by.

But when they got to the Hoofbeats of History stable, Jackie wasn't there.

"Oh, no," said Jessie to the man who came out to meet them. "She was supposed to give us a tour."

The man smiled. He was medium height, with shoulder-length brown hair, and he wore sunglasses. "Then you must be the Aldens. I'm Mike Carson, Jackie's partner. She couldn't be here, so she arranged for me to give you a special tour."

"That sounds great," said Henry. "My name's Henry and these are my sisters, Jessie and Violet, and my brother Benny."

Mike led them toward a black carriage with silver trim. A big, sandy-colored horse stood hitched to it.

"Welcome to Hoofbeats of History," Mike said. He nodded toward the horse. "This is Sugar. Not only did Jackie leave the very best tour guide in charge but she left the very best horse."

"Is she called Sugar because she is a sweet horse?" asked Jessie, patting Sugar's soft nose.

"Because she's sweet *and* she likes to be fed lumps of sugar," said Mike.

"Watch, our dog, is called Watch because he is a good watchdog," said Benny.

"Hello, Watch," said Mike, scratching Watch's ears. Then he motioned toward the carriage. "Now, all aboard."

The Aldens and Mrs. Ashleigh got in the carriage. Benny held tightly to Watch's leash.

"Okay, Sugar, let's go," said Mike, and Sugar pulled the carriage out into the streets of Charleston.

"Look at all the people!" said Benny as they drove up one narrow street and down another. He waved at people as Sugar trotted by. "It's like being in a parade." Benny loved parades.

"Look at all the beautiful houses," Violet breathed. She pointed at fences made of iron shaped into delicate patterns. "It looks like lace made of iron," she said.

Mrs. Ashleigh laughed and nodded. "That's a very good description, Violet."

As they drove, Mike told them that Charleston had been built in the middle of a marsh and behind walls to protect it from enemy attack. "The name *Charleston* comes from Charles Town, after the English King Charles II," he explained.

He showed them the high-water marks that the sea had left behind after the last hurricane. The water had been taller than Benny, taller than Jessie, even taller than Grandfather.

"But Charleston is used to hurricanes," he said. "And earthquakes, too."

"That's what Diana told us," said Henry. "She said San Francisco had lots of earthquakes, but that Charleston had had them, too."

"Well, I don't know Diana, but she's right. In 1886 we had an earthquake that lasted eight minutes!" Mike said.

"That won't happen again soon, will it?" asked Violet, looking a little nervous.

"I don't think so," said Mike. "I hope not!"

They drove past the City Market, where people once shopped for food, "just like in a big, open grocery store," Mike told them. Now the market was the center of restaurants and shops and artists of all kinds. Women sat on corners and wove beautiful baskets of palmetto, bulrush, pine, and sweetgrass, "a craft brought by their great-great-grandmothers from Africa and the Caribbean and handed down for generations from mother to daughter," Mike told them. "Some of those baskets are in the Smithsonian Museum in Washington, D.C. They are works of art and are worth a lot of money."

At the end of the tour, the Aldens thanked Mike, and Sugar, too. "I've lived all my life in Charleston," said Mrs. Ashleigh, "but I've never been on a tour before. I learned a lot of new things."

"You should give tours dressed as a pirate," said Benny.

"That's a great idea, Benny," said Mike. "Maybe I will."

As they walked away from the stable, Mike called after them, "Are you going home now?"

"Not just yet," said Grandfather. "I think we'll go get some ice cream."

"Good," said Benny.

"The best ice cream is over by the market," said Mike. "It'll take a little while to walk there, but it'll be worth it. And you can see more of Charleston."

"Thank you, Mike," said Mr. Alden.

"Take your time in Charleston," Mike urged. "There is a lot to see and do."

"We will," said Jessie cheerfully. "After all, we're on a holiday today!"

Grandfather Alden and Mrs. Ashleigh dropped the children off at the house before going to the hardware store for supplies.

When they got back, Henry said, "I think we should take a look in the study, don't you, Jessie and Violet?"

"Yes," said Jessie.

"Yes," said Violet. "Come on, Benny."

She and Jessie and Henry wanted Benny to find his made-up pirate map so they could go on their treasure hunt.

But when they pushed the door of the study open, they stopped in shock.

"Oh, no!" cried Violet. "What happened?"

CHAPTER 6

Gold Coins and Iron Bars

"Everything's a mess!" said Jessie.

The piles of neatly stacked papers were scattered everywhere, all over the study.

"Look!" said Benny. He pointed. "The wind must have blown through the open window."

"It couldn't have, Benny. We didn't leave the window open," said Henry. "Someone must have opened it and climbed through."

Jessie went over to the window and bent

to examine it. "You're right," she said.
"See?" The others crowded around her and
stared at a black smudge on the recently
painted windowsill. "That looks like a dirty,
smeared footprint," said Jessie.

"All our hard work! Why would someone
do such an awful thing?" said Violet.

"Maybe it was Mrs. Ashleigh's son.
Maybe he came and did it to scare her so she
would sell the house," said Jessie.

"No! I know what they were doing," said
Benny. "They were looking for a map for
Mr. Fitzhugh's pirate treasure! They were
going to steal it!"

"How do you know that, Benny?" asked
Henry.

"Because they didn't find it. Here it is,"
Benny answered triumphantly.

Benny picked a piece of paper up off the
floor from just beneath the edge of the desk.
He held it up.

It was the pretend map that Henry had
made.

"It *is* a map, Benny. But maybe not

the map the thief was looking for."

"It's a pirate's map," insisted Benny. "It has a skull and crossbones in it, just like in my books about pirates. And there's an X marking where the treasure is."

Benny frowned. "But it has my name on it, too." He studied the map for a long moment, then slowly read aloud, "Benny's Pirate Map."

He looked up at Henry and laughed. "You can't fool me," said Benny. "That's a map *you* made. It's not a real one."

"It's a pretend map," said Jessie, laughing, too. "But there is a real treasure at the end of it."

"Gold?" asked Benny.

"Not exactly," said Violet.

"Oh, boy," said Benny. "Let's go on our treasure hunt right now."

Henry looked around at the messy study. "Well, we might as well. We don't have any good clues to the mystery here."

The Aldens quickly put the papers back in boxes so they could sort them again later.

Then they set out on Benny's treasure hunt.

Benny was the leader. He held the map and, with Violet's help, found the way. Watch ran ahead, sniffing and barking as they read the map.

"There's a big tree drawn here," said Benny. He looked at the map, then looked up and pointed. "There it is. We turn toward the sunrise by the tree, it says."

He wrinkled his brow for a moment when they reached the tree, trying to figure out the clue. Then he said, "The sun rises over there. So we go that way!"

"Oops, Benny, you almost missed a clue," said Henry.

Benny stopped so quickly that his older brother almost ran into him. He held the map up. "What clue?" he asked.

"Light house on the left, green house ahead," read Henry.

"Oh!" said Benny. He turned and looked at the houses in the dunes until he saw a green one. He led the way across the dunes toward it.

On and on they followed the map.

Once, Jessie stopped and looked back over her shoulder.

"What is it?" asked Violet. "What do you see?"

"I had the funniest feeling . . . as if we were being followed. And I thought I saw someone in a gray raincoat. But I don't see anybody now."

"Why would someone follow us?" asked Violet.

Jessie shrugged. "I don't know. Maybe it was just my imagination."

They came at last to the dunes near the beach. Henry leaned over and clipped Watch's leash on. "To keep Watch from smelling the treasure and beating us to it," he explained.

"We're almost there," said Benny. "We've almost reached the treasure!" Holding the map high, he ran ahead onto the narrow walkway made of boards that led through the dunes to the beach.

Benny's footsteps clattered on the boards

as he hurried to find the treasure.

Suddenly someone leaped out of the dunes by the walkway and grabbed the map.

"Hey!" shouted Benny. "Stop!"

But it was too late. The mysterious figure jerked the map from Benny's hands and ran into the dunes and disappeared!

"Help!" cried Benny. "Stop, thief!"

"Benny's in trouble," said Henry. "Come on!"

They ran down the walkway. But Benny was nowhere in sight.

Henry cupped his hands to his mouth. "Benny!" he shouted. "Benny, where are you?"

Suddenly Watch tugged at his leash. He pulled Jessie to one side of the walkway.

"Footprints," said Jessie, pointing. "Good dog, Watch." They jumped into the sand and began to follow the footsteps.

They hadn't gone far when they heard someone shouting.

"It's Benny! He's over there," said Violet. With Watch straining at the leash, they ran as fast as they could through the sand.

And there was Benny, standing at the top of a sand dune with his hands in fists. He was scowling and his face was very red.

"Benny! Are you all right? What happened?" asked Jessie.

"Somebody stole the map," wailed Benny. "And he got away."

"What did the person look like?" asked Violet.

"He was wearing a big gray raincoat, and he had a brown ponytail. That's all I saw," said Benny. "I couldn't even tell if it was a man or a woman."

"A gray raincoat!" exclaimed Jessie. "Then I *was* right." Quickly she told Henry and Benny about the person she thought had been following them.

"But why would anybody follow us?" asked Henry. "And why would anyone steal a map that wasn't even real?"

"Because he wants to steal *my* treasure," said Benny. "Hurry. We have to get there before the thief does."

"I think the thief knows that the map isn't real by now, Benny," said Jessie. "He probably won't risk coming back."

"But I remember exactly where your treasure is hidden," said Henry. "We can still go find it."

He led the way to a small tree near the boardwalk in the dunes and pointed. An X had been drawn on the trunk of the tree with white chalk.

"X marks the spot," cried Benny happily. With Watch's help he'd soon dug up a small cookie tin. "Gold!" said Benny when he took the top off the tin. Inside were some gold-wrapped chocolate coins that Jessie had bought at the island grocery store.

They ate some of the treasure as they walked home. All except Watch. "Chocolate is bad for dogs, Watch. Remember?" Benny told Watch.

As they walked and ate their treasure, they talked about the map thief.

"If someone thought that was a real treasure map, then someone really believes there is a pirate's treasure," said Jessie. "Maybe that's why he broke into the study."

"But Diana said nobody believes that there's a treasure," Violet reminded them. "She said it was just a story."

"Maybe she said that to throw us off guard," said Henry. "She *did* say she needed money."

"She knew we weren't going to be home, too. Remember? We waved at her as we drove away this morning," said Violet.

Jessie said, "So did Jackie. She's the one who invited us on the tour this morning. Maybe she's the one who thinks that there is a treasure. Maybe she knows more than she's telling us."

"Like a secret about the buried treasure?" asked Benny.

"It could be," Henry said.

"But she couldn't be the one who was following us," said Violet. "She has short black hair. The person in the gray raincoat had a brown ponytail."

"Just like Diana," said Henry.

They walked in silence, peeling the gold foil off the chocolate coins and eating them, and thinking about the mystery. But when they reached Mrs. Ashleigh's house, they were no nearer a solution.

"Is this another mystery?" asked Benny happily.

"It sure looks that way, Benny," said Henry.

"I wonder what will happen next," said Violet.

She got her answer that very night.

CHAPTER 7

Who's There?

I'm thirsty, thought Violet sleepily, waking from a deep sleep. It was very late. Violet got her flashlight and water glass from by the bed and went to the bathroom to fill the glass.

Back in her room, she sat down on the edge of her bed, turned off the flashlight, and took a sip of cool water.

Suddenly she heard a funny sound outside.

Violet stood up and peered out her window. She had the room above the kitchen. It looked out over the side yard, where the Pirate's Gate had once hung.

The Pirate's Gate wasn't there now, of course.

But someone in a raincoat was.

Quickly Violet grabbed her flashlight and ran out of her room into Jessie's. "Jessie," she gasped.

"Uhh," said Jessie sleepily.

"Someone's outside in the garden. I think it's the person who took Benny's map! Tell Henry and Benny," said Violet as she hurried away.

That woke Jessie up. In no time at all she'd gotten Henry and Benny and Watch. "Don't bark, Watch," warned Benny. They ran through the house as fast and as quietly as they could, trying not to wake Mrs. Ashleigh or Grandfather Alden.

They raced to the kitchen. Henry, who was the tallest, peered through a window that looked out over the garden.

A shadowy figure stood only a few feet away.

Suddenly the figure moved. It raised its arm and they all heard a dull clang, clang, like metal on metal.

Watch growled very softly, but he didn't bark.

"What is he doing?" whispered Violet.

"I don't know," said Henry. "We've got to see who it is. Maybe if we surprise him we can at least see his face."

They ran to the kitchen door and threw it open.

"Stop!" cried Henry. "Who's there? Who are you?"

The shadowy figure whirled and leaped through the opening where the gate had once hung. He went so fast that they didn't even have time to train their flashlights on him.

"Did you recognize anything?" asked Henry.

"Just that raincoat," Jessie said.

"What was he doing?" said Violet. She

turned her flashlight on the iron fence and got her answer. "Oh, no!" she said. "Look."

The intruder had hit one of the hinges where the gate had hung. When Mr. Farrier had fixed it, it had looked shiny and new. Now it was scratched and dented.

"Why would anyone do that?" Henry wondered aloud. He bent forward to inspect the damaged hinge. "It's not bad," he said at last. "Mostly scratched. You could still hang the gate on it."

"Oh, good," said Benny.

"It doesn't make sense," Henry concluded. "Why would anyone vandalize Mrs. Ashleigh's fence?"

"Maybe it's her son, trying to scare her into moving," said Jessie slowly. "And maybe he *is* the one who snuck in to steal the papers. Too bad we didn't get a better look at him."

"See?" said Benny. "Mr. Ashleigh *is* a mean man."

"We don't know *who* it was, Benny," Violet reminded her younger brother. "It

looked like the man from this afternoon."

"Or woman," said Jessie, thinking of Diana. "We just don't know."

"Maybe Diana and Forrest Ashleigh are working together," said Henry. "After all, she lives nearby. It would be easy for her to get to Mrs. Ashleigh's house without being noticed. All we know is that it was the person in the raincoat."

"And whoever it was knows his way around. That's one of the reasons he got away," said Henry.

The four children looked at each other.

The clues were beginning to add up. But they still weren't sure why all these mysterious things had happened. That was the biggest mystery of all.

"I'm going to Charleston to see about the gate and to take care of some business," said Mrs. Ashleigh a couple of days later, coming out onto the front porch.

The Aldens had finished repairing the porch and had even added new steps to re-

place the stump. Now they were painting.
"I don't suppose anybody would like to come
with me," Mrs. Ashleigh went on.

"Me!" said Benny, dropping his paint-
brush.

"I think we'd all like to go visit Mr. Farrier's studio," said Jessie.

The Aldens changed out of their porch-
painting clothes, and soon they were on their
way to Charleston.

Many people were still working to clean
up after the hurricane. "We can't waste time
here," said Mrs. Ashleigh with a rueful
smile. "You never know when the next hurricane will hit."

Mr. Farrier's shop was a low brick building
not far from the Hoofbeats of History carriage tours stable. Inside, they found Mr.
Farrier hard at work hammering a piece of
red-hot iron into a curved shape. He wore a
hat and safety goggles and gloves. The hammer rang against the hot metal with a dull
clang, clang sound. Sometimes sparks flew
up when the hammer hit the iron.

When he'd finished shaping the iron, he dipped it into a nearby bucket of water to cool it off, then put it down carefully. He pushed back his safety goggles, took off his gloves, and came over to shake hands.

"Mrs. Ashleigh. I'm glad to see you. I need to talk to you about that gate," said Mr. Farrier.

"Can't it be fixed?" asked Mrs. Ashleigh in a worried voice.

"Oh, yes, it can be fixed. But . . ." He stopped and looked around at the four children. "Anyway, if I could have a word with you in private."

Mrs. Ashleigh said, "Of course. But I have an appointment at the bank right now."

"Could we stay and watch Mr. Farrier work?" asked Jessie. "Just for a little while."

"If it's all right with Mr. Farrier. Then you can walk down to the bank to meet me."

Mr. Farrier nodded. "You're welcome to stay for a little while, and I can give you directions to the bank," he said. "Just don't get too close to the fire or the hot metal.

You'll have to sit over there." He pointed to an iron bench along one brick wall.

The Aldens readily agreed.

As Mr. Farrier worked, he told the children about how he had learned his skill from his father, who had learned it from his father before him. "My great-great-great-grandfather was a slave," said Mr. Farrier matter-of-factly. "But he was so good at making wrought-iron and cast-iron designs for fences and balconies that he was able to buy his freedom with the money he made. He set up his own shop and soon had more business than he could handle. You can still see some of his work around town today. It's famous and very valuable."

Mr. Farrier poured molten iron into hollow molds shaped like rosettes and stars. "The same as putting cake batter into a cake pan," he explained. "I have molds in all different sizes and shapes. When the iron cools, it hardens and I remove the mold. Then I'll have an iron decoration shaped like the mold. That's called cast iron, and it can be hollow or solid."

He pointed to the bench they were sitting on. "That's cast iron. I make molds of different sections and weld them together. But the bench also has some wrought iron, which is shaped by hand."

"What is the Pirate's Gate?" asked Henry.

Mr. Farrier gave Henry a sharp look. "Not much of the Pirate's Gate was made with molds — it's mostly wrought iron. You kids really are interested in that gate, aren't you?"

As he worked, Mr. Farrier asked the Aldens what they knew about the Pirate's Gate. He seemed very uneasy and kept checking the back door of the studio to make sure it was locked.

"What are you making?" asked Benny.

"Window grills," said Mr. Farrier. "You put them in front of windows and people can't break in."

"Who are they for?" asked Jessie.

"Me," said Mr. Farrier. He jerked his head

toward the windows of his shop. Seeing their surprised looks, he said, "Someone tried to break in last night. He got scared away, but better safe than sorry."

"It would be hard to steal your ironwork," said Violet. "It's so heavy."

Mr. Farrier shrugged.

"I guess we'd better go meet Mrs. Ashleigh," said Jessie. "Thank you, Mr. Farrier."

"You're welcome," said Mr. Farrier. He gave them directions to the bank and the Aldens left.

They'd almost reached the bank when Jessie grabbed Henry's arm. "Look," she said. "It's him!"

CHAPTER 8

The Mysterious Stranger

Up ahead, Forrest Ashleigh, Mrs. Ashleigh's son, had just come out of the bank. He looked like a banker himself in his dark suit and tie.

But it wasn't Mr. Ashleigh that Jessie was pointing toward. It was the person in the gray raincoat. He — or she — was in the shadows, leaning against the side of a building. The person raised a hand and signaled Mr. Ashleigh to come over. Mr. Ashleigh looked around, scowled, and then walked to-ward the stranger.

"We have to get closer," said Henry. "We have to see who that is."

Trying to act as if nothing were wrong, the four children walked casually toward the bank.

"Don't stare, Benny," said Jessie. "It looks suspicious."

"I'm not," said Benny, keeping his gaze fastened on Mr. Ashleigh and the stranger.

"So Mr. Ashleigh knows the stranger," said Jessie. "Hmm. Very interesting."

"Very suspicious, if you ask me," said Henry.

Violet said, "I don't think Mr. Ashleigh *ever* smiles. He is always frowning when we see him."

Mr. Ashleigh shook his head. He folded his arms. The stranger pointed toward the bank. Mr. Ashleigh shook his head again.

Just then a voice said, "Henry! Jessie! Vi-olet! Benny! Over here!" Mrs. Ashleigh came down the steps of the bank toward the Aldens.

As she did, the stranger turned and ducked quickly down the alley by the building. Mr. Ashleigh looked over his shoulder at his mother.

She saw him and waved. "Forrest! Come over here. I want you to meet someone."

Grudgingly, her son came over to join them. "Forrest works in this bank," she said. "He's vice president!"

Forrest Ashleigh shook hands with each of the Aldens and said hello. "I hear you've been helping my mother with Hurricane Heap," he said.

"Hurricane Heap?" asked Violet.

Forrest smiled unexpectedly at Violet. When he did, he looked a lot like his mother. And a lot nicer than he had seemed earlier. At least, that's what Violet thought.

"It's what I call the old house. Oh, it's a nice old house and I love it. But sooner or later it's going to blow away in a hurricane and then what will be left?"

"It's been around a lot longer than you or I have," said Mrs. Ashleigh.

Forrest looked as if he wanted to argue, but he didn't. Instead he said, "Well, nice to meet you. Thanks for helping Mother with Hurricane Heap. I just hope another hurricane doesn't come along and blow you away before you finish cleaning up the mess from this one!"

Henry cleared his throat. "Mr. Ashleigh? Who were you talking to just then?"

Forrest Ashleigh paused. He frowned again. Suddenly he didn't look so friendly. "Nobody," he said, after a long moment. "That is, nobody I knew. It was just someone who asked me the time."

Still frowning, he turned on his heel and left.

The Aldens painted the railings of the porch all afternoon. As they painted, they talked about the mystery.

"I think someone is definitely after the pirate's treasure," Benny insisted. "The gold that Mr. Ashleigh buried. *Not* Mrs. Ashleigh's son," he added. "Mr. Ashleigh the pirate."

"I think so, too," said Jessie. "This all started when we were helping Mrs. Ashleigh go through those boxes of papers for the museum."

"But there is no map in the papers," said Henry. "We have been all through them. There is nothing that looks like a treasure map."

"Maybe there's some other clue," said Violet. "A clue that leads to the map. Or the treasure."

"Maybe the map is drawn in invisible ink!" said Benny.

"Maybe, Benny," said Jessie. "But I don't think so."

"As soon as we finish painting, we'll go through the papers again," said Henry. "Maybe we will see a clue that we missed."

They had just finished painting for the day when Mr. Farrier's red truck pulled up in front of the house. "Hello," he said. "I finished repairing the gate and brought it back. Is Mrs. Ashleigh here?"

"No," said Violet. "But she will be back soon. She just went to the post office and the grocery store."

Mr. Farrier didn't look happy when he heard that.

"You could hang the gate while you wait," suggested Henry. "We can help you."

Shaking his head, Mr. Farrier said, "No. I think I'll put the gate around back." He hoisted the gate out of the truck and put it on a hand truck. Then he wheeled it around to the back of the house.

"What happened here?" he called a few minutes later. He stopped at the fence where the gate had hung and pointed at the hinge.

"Someone came in the night and vandalized the fence," Jessie explained. To her surprise, Mr. Farrier didn't seem at all shocked.

He took his glasses off and polished them on his shirtsleeve. "Hmmm," he said. "Interesting. Well, I can fix that hinge in no time."

The blacksmith was as good as his word. In no time at all, the hinge was like new. "But don't hang that gate up until I talk to Mrs. Ashleigh. Don't even touch it," he warned. He looked at his watch. "I can't wait any longer. Please tell her to call me as soon as possible. It's urgent!" He got into his truck, slammed the door, and drove away.

"Mr. Farrier is acting *weird*," said Jessie.

"Yes," said Violet. "As if he thinks we'll hurt the Pirate's Gate. But why would we do that?"

"Did you notice that he wasn't at all surprised when we told him about the vandal?" Jessie asked.

Henry nodded. "I noticed that, too. You don't think Mr. Farrier did it, do you?"

"Why would he do that? He just had to fix it again," said Benny.

Jessie said slowly, "Maybe we are wrong. Maybe the mystery didn't start when we began to go through those old papers. Maybe the mystery started *before* that."

"What do you mean, Jessie?" asked Violet.

"I mean, maybe the mystery started when we solved that first mystery — when we found the Pirate's Gate," she answered. "Come on. I think it's time we looked at those papers again."

The Boxcar Children cleaned the paintbrushes and put everything away. Then they washed up and went back to the study.

"What are we looking for?" Henry asked Jessie.

"I'm not sure," said Jessie. "But someone really wants the Pirate's Gate. Maybe there's something in these papers that will tell us why."

"Do you think a clue to the buried treasure might be hidden *in* the gate?" asked Violet.

"Maybe," said Jessie.

"A treasure gate," said Benny. "Like that bridge where Diana used to live."

"What are you talking about, Benny?" asked Henry, pulling a folder out of a pile on the desk. "Here. Here are the plans for the house and the gate."

"What bridge, Benny?" said Violet.

"You know. That gold bridge," said Benny. "With the earthquakes."

"Oh." Jessie laughed. "You mean the Golden Gate Bridge, Benny. The Golden Gate . . ." her voice trailed off. Her eyes got wide.

"That's it," she cried.

"It is?" asked Benny. "Have I solved another mystery?"

"I think you have," said Jessie, giving him a hug.

She bent over the plans spread out on the desk. They all stared at them.

"What is it, Jessie? Have you found the treasure?" asked Henry.

"Yes," said Jessie dramatically. She pointed at the design for the Pirate's Gate. "Right there!"

CHAPTER 9

A Treasure Trap

"Mr. Farrier said the gate was mostly wrought iron, remember?" said Jessie. "But it's not. It's cast iron. See all these molds? That's how Mr. Farrier said cast iron was made — by pouring molten iron into molds."

"Like cake batter into a cake pan," remembered Benny.

"Right," said Jessie.

"How could Mr. Farrier make a mistake like that?" asked Violet.

"He didn't," said Henry, who'd been studying the gate design intently. "He just didn't want to tell us that he'd discovered the secret of the gate." He pointed to the design. "Old Mr. Fitzhugh made cast-iron molds — hollow ones — and filled them up with *gold*. It says so right here."

"Where?" asked Benny. "Where does it say gold?"

"It doesn't say gold, Benny," explained Jessie. "But look. It does say, 'Molds received and filled by F. Fitzhugh.' "

"Why would Mr. Fitzhugh want hollow molds? Why would he want to fill them himself unless he had something to hide?"

"That's exactly it," said Jessie. "And the only parts of the gate that weren't cast iron were the outer decorations and parts. Look what it says above the design: 'Fill and hang.' "

"Fill the hollow gate and hang it," translated Violet in an awed voice. "He poured it full of molten gold, just like we saw Mr.

Farrier do with the cast-iron molds at his studio."

"Pirate's treasure!" cried Benny. "Pirate's gold!"

"The gold, the gold, we found the gold!" said Violet. Watch barked and pranced around.

"Let's go get the gate," said Benny.

"And tell Mrs. Ashleigh," said Jessie.

"Wait!" Henry cried.

They all looked at him in surprise.

"We've solved the mystery of the Pirate's Gate," said Henry. "But we haven't solved the mystery of who else knows that the gate is the key to the treasure."

"Mr. Farrier knows. That's why he didn't hang the gate back up," said Violet. "He must have discovered it when he was fixing it. That's what made it so important for him to talk to Mrs. Ashleigh. So he could tell her."

"And whoever tried to break into Mr. Farrier's shop knows, too," said Jessie. "Remember? That's why he was making iron grills for his windows. Because someone had tried to break in."

Henry said, "Of course! And that's why he asked us so many questions. He wanted to know if we knew."

"If we hang it up, I think whoever is after the gate will come back for it," said Jessie. "I think they've been following us, watching us. They'll see us put the gate up. They'll think we haven't figured out its secret."

"Yes. We'll hang the gate. We'll set a trap and catch the thief," said Henry.

The Boxcar Children hurried downstairs. They discovered that Mr. Farrier had opened the kitchen door and leaned the gate against the wall inside.

They looked at the gate with new eyes. It was hard to believe it was made of gold. The cast iron was pretty and graceful. No sign of gold or treasure showed anywhere.

Very carefully, the four Aldens lifted the gate up and carried it out to the fence. It was heavy, so they had to stop and rest twice. But at last the gate was mounted on its hinges.

"There," said Jessie in a satisfied voice. "Now the trap is set. All we have to do is watch and wait."

"It's getting late," said Henry. "Almost nighttime. I think the thief will come tonight."

Just then thunder rumbled overhead. They looked up to see the sky filling with clouds. A gust of wind blew, and then another, stronger gust. With the third gust, the wind was blowing steadily. Lightning flashed across the ominous clouds.

Mrs. Ashleigh drove up to the house and got out. Grandfather was with her.

"We have good news," Jessie began.

"Not now, Jessie," said Mrs. Ashleigh. She didn't even seem to notice the gate. Her face was worried. "Hurry into the house. We have to get ready. Another hurricane may be on its way!"

"We have a lot of work to do to get ready

for it in case it does come," added Grand-father. "And not much time!"

After that, they didn't stop moving for a minute. Mrs. Ashleigh checked her supplies to make sure she had plenty of fresh water and flashlight batteries. She told the Aldens to pack up their things, in case they had to evacuate the island. Then they went around closing shutters over the windows and mov-ing things from outside into the house.

Meanwhile, the wind grew louder and stronger. It howled across the narrow, flat island. Rain began to fall in sheets.

"My hat!" cried Henry as the wind blew it away. The hat flew into the air and whirled out of sight before Henry could even chase it.

"The shutters are all up," said Grand-father. "Time to go inside."

They gathered around the kitchen table to eat dinner and watch the weather news on the small television that Mrs. Ashleigh kept there.

"What began as a minor storm in the Caribbean has been growing steadily stronger as it moves up the coast," the weather announcer said. She was standing at the foot of a pier, wearing a raincoat. Behind her, angry waves lashed the pilings and sent spray high into the air. "It has now crossed Florida and reached Georgia. Winds of over a hundred miles per hour have been reported. Residents along the coast of Georgia are being evacuated." The picture changed to show cars creeping down an interstate highway. Along the edges of the highway, trees whipped back and forth in the wind.

"Are we going to have to evacuate like that?" asked Benny, his eyes huge.

"We'll know in another hour or two," said Mrs. Ashleigh calmly. "Now let's make sure all of our flashlights are working. Here are extra batteries in case we need them. There's a flashlight for everyone."

Something banged hard against the side of the house. Watch began to bark and Benny jumped. "W-what is that?" he asked. "Is it the hurricane?"

"It sounds as if a shutter has come loose," said Grandfather. "Henry, will you come help me fasten it down?"

Hearing how calm his grandfather sounded, Benny was a little less worried about the storm. When Watch whimpered, he said, "Don't worry, Watch. I won't let anything happen to you. If the storm gets too bad, we will leave. Won't we, Mrs. Ashleigh?"

"Of course, dear," answered Mrs. Ashleigh.

Even though they wore raincoats and hats and boots, Grandfather and Henry were soaking wet when they came back inside.

On the television, the announcer appeared in front of a map showing where the hurricane was.

"It looks awfully close to us," said Violet.

"The hurricane is moving closer to the South Carolina coast," said the announcer. "Residents may have to begin evacuation procedures. Stay tuned — "

Just then the lights all flickered and went out.

"Oh, no!" cried Benny. Then he hugged Watch and said, "Don't worry, boy. We have flashlights."

Even as Benny spoke, Mrs. Ashleigh turned her flashlight on. Then she lit candles and set them in the middle of the table. She gave flashlights to Henry and Grandfather Alden so they could go to their bedrooms and change into dry clothes.

"When you come back down," Mrs. Ashleigh said, "we'll get a puzzle out of the closet and put it together at the kitchen table by candlelight."

"Sort of like camping out and sitting around a campfire," said Jessie bravely.

"May I pick out the puzzle?" asked Benny.

Mrs. Ashleigh nodded. "Take a flashlight to the den. The puzzles are in the cabinet there."

"I know where they are," said Violet. "Jessie and I brought them back downstairs and put them there."

"You can come help me and Watch pick out a puzzle, then," said Benny. The walk from the kitchen to the den in the dark, with the storm roaring outside, was a little scary. But now that Violet was coming with him, Benny wasn't worried. He turned on his flashlight and pointed it down the hallway. "Just follow me."

When Benny and Violet returned to the kitchen, Henry and Grandfather were sitting at the kitchen table.

"We picked out a good puzzle," said Benny. "With five hundred pieces."

"It's a picture of a garden," added Violet, thinking of the Pirate's Gate on the fence by the garden outside.

Jessie, who was standing near the kitchen window, leaned over to look out. But the shutters had been closed and she couldn't see anything. She began to worry. What if the thief came and stole the gate in the middle of the hurricane? They wouldn't even be able to hear it.

As if reading her thoughts, Henry said,

"No one could be out in weather like this, could they, Grandfather? The wind is blowing too hard."

"I don't think so," said Grandfather.

Jessie didn't think so, either. But still, she decided to listen very, very carefully for the thief, just in case.

Mrs. Ashleigh finished putting batteries in the radio and set it on the kitchen counter. They listened as the announcer said, "Still no decision to evacuate . . ."

Then Mrs. Ashleigh turned the puzzle upside down on the table. "Let's get to work on this puzzle," she said.

Outside, the storm screamed and howled. Rain battered the house and rattled against the shutters. But inside the house, in the flickering light of the candles, the Boxcar Children were able to stay calm and brave. As the hours passed, even Watch settled down, curling up beneath Benny's feet as Benny sorted out pieces of the puzzle and fit them into place.

Then suddenly Watch raised his head.

Henry looked up. "Do you hear that?" he asked.

Violet looked up, too. She cocked her head. "It's not as noisy," she said. "Is the storm going away?"

"I think it is," said Grandfather.

Mrs. Ashleigh reached over and fiddled with the dials of the radio. Static crackled through the air. Then the announcer's voice said, "The hurricane has veered away from the coast. It is going out to sea. Evacuation will not be necessary. Stay tuned for further details."

Benny dropped the puzzle piece he was holding. "Is the hurricane gone?" he said.

"Almost," said Jessie.

"Hooray!" said Benny. "Hooray! Do you hear that, Watch? We don't have to worry anymore."

But Watch didn't agree. He ran out from under the table and leaped at the kitchen door and began to bark with all his might.

CHAPTER 10

Stop, Thief!

Jessie jumped to her feet. "It's the trap!" she cried. "Quick, open the door!"

Grandfather and Mrs. Ashleigh looked very surprised as the four Aldens rushed toward the kitchen door. "Everyone get a flashlight," said Henry.

"Hurry! Or they'll get away!" Violet said.

"What's going on?" asked Grandfather Alden.

"We've found the pirate's treasure," said

Benny. "Only someone's trying to steal it."

With Grandfather and Mrs. Ashleigh right behind them, the Boxcar Children rushed out of the kitchen door and through the backyard toward the gate.

Henry led the way to the door. "We set a trap to catch a thief," he said over his shoulder.

They all turned their flashlights toward the gate.

"It's gone!" cried Violet. "Oh, no! It's gone!"

"Look. There it is!" gasped Jessie, pointing with the beam of her flashlight through the rain and wind.

In front of the house, two figures were struggling to lift the gate into the back of a blue van.

"Stop! Stop, thief!" shouted Henry, running as fast as he could.

Barking madly, Watch ran, too. He leaped up and caught the pants leg of one of the thieves.

"Oww! No! Get away!" a woman's voice shouted. She kicked at Watch and tripped.

The other thief dropped his end of the gate into the mud and began to run. The woman fell, still holding onto the gate. The gate tipped over on her, trapping her in a puddle.

But Henry caught the escaping thief by one arm and Jessie caught him by the other. "Oh, no, you don't," said Henry. "You were trying to steal our gate."

"No! Let me go," the man said.

"It's Jackie," gasped Violet, bending over the woman. "Jackie James! Oh dear! Are you hurt?" Violet tried to lift the gate off Jackie, but it was too heavy.

"No, I'm not hurt! Mike Carson, don't you dare leave me here like this," cried Jackie, struggling to get out from under the gate. "This is all your fault!"

"Mike Carson? Jackie's partner?" said Mrs. Ashleigh. "Jackie, Mike, what's going on?" She looked completely bewildered.

It was indeed Mike. He stopped trying to

pull free from Henry and Jessie. His shoulders slumped. Slowly he turned to face the Aldens and Mrs. Ashleigh.

"Someone get me out of here," said Jackie. She was still caught beneath one side of the gate. She was covered with mud. Her rain hat had blown off and her hair was stuck to her head. She looked angry.

"We can't stay out here," said Henry. "I think we'd better go in the house."

"Yes," agreed Grandfather Alden. "I'd like to hear what's going on."

"I would, too!" exclaimed Mrs. Ashleigh.

"Don't try to run away," Benny warned as he helped his grandfather and Violet and Mrs. Ashleigh lift the gate off Jackie.

Watch barked.

"I won't," said Jackie angrily. She scrambled to her feet.

She stalked ahead of them into the house. Looking sheepish, Mike picked up one end of the gate and helped the Boxcar Children carry it.

"We should put it inside the kitchen door," said Jessie. "So no one can try to steal it again."

They carried the gate inside and leaned it carefully against the wall while Mrs. Ashleigh got towels so everybody could begin to rub themselves dry.

Henry pointed to the chairs and said to Jackie James and Mike Carson, "You can sit down if you like."

"Thanks," said Mike.

"Humph!" said Jackie, reluctantly sitting beside him and folding her arms.

"I think we should all sit down," said Grandfather Alden. "Ellen and I would like to know what's going on."

"We found the treasure," Benny burst out. "Mr. Fitzhugh's pirate treasure!"

Mrs. Ashleigh shook her head. "Oh, Benny. That's not possible. That's just an old story that people made up. It's not really true."

"Yes, it is," said Jessie. "Mr. Fitzhugh really did hide a treasure. He hid it where

he could see it anytime he wanted. You've been looking at it every day your whole life, too."

Wrinkling her brow and looking confused, Mrs. Ashleigh said, "What are you talking about?"

Violet pointed at the Pirate's Gate. "It's there. It's in the Pirate's Gate. The Pirate's Gate is made of gold!"

Mrs. Ashleigh's mouth dropped open in amazement. "Made of gold? That's impossible," she said.

Jackie burst out, "It would have been mine. I was so close! How did you know? How did you figure it out?"

Jessie folded her arms. "First you tell us how you knew about the gate."

"I didn't right away," said Jackie sulkily. "I thought there might be more truth to the legends of Mr. Fitzhugh's pirate's treasure than most people believed, but I didn't connect it to the gate."

"But weren't you trying to steal it when we first found you and Diana putting it into the truck that day?" asked Jessie.

"That gate is a valuable antique in its own right. When the high tides of the hurricane washed it into my yard, I knew that I could sell it for a lot of money to an antiques dealer who wouldn't ask any questions about where it came from. Then my money problems would be over." She frowned at the Aldens. The shadows from the candles flickered across her face. "Diana offered to help me with it. But she didn't recognize the gate. She's just a carpenter! And then, as I was loading it into the truck, I realized it wasn't just an old wrought-iron gate. There was something funny about it, something that I couldn't put my finger on. A little piece of the ship had been chipped away, leaving a little hollow place. But before I could take the gate away safely — "

"We came along," said Violet. "And made you give the gate back to Mrs. Ashleigh. That's why you were so rude to us."

Jackie shrugged. "I still didn't realize what that gate was made of. I thought that something in the design of it was a clue to where the treasure was hidden. Or maybe that a clue or map was actually hidden in the hollow ship. I knew the ship was cast iron and thought it sounded hollow when I accidentally banged it against my truck."

She glanced over at the gate, then looked away as if it pained her to look at it. She went on, "Because I'm a history buff, I knew that Ellen had papers dating back from Mr. Fitzhugh's time, including plans for the house and designs for the gate. I thought if I could just get a look at those papers, I might be able to piece together the clues, come up with a map for the treasure."

"So you invited us to a carriage tour and broke into the house while we were gone," said Violet.

"Yes," Jackie said.

Mike said, "I was supposed to keep you busy while I searched." He glanced at Jackie.

"When I opened the window and climbed through," Jackie continued, "I accidentally knocked most of the papers off the desk. A gust of wind came through and did the rest. I barely had time to find the design and start tracing a copy when you came back."

"With Mike following us. Dressed in a gray raincoat, right?" guessed Jessie.

"Yeah," Mike said. "I heard you say something about a treasure hunt and a map. So I followed you and stole the map. But it wasn't a real map."

Jackie gave him a disgusted look.

Mike sighed. "I'm Jackie's partner in the tour guide business," he said. "And in the hunt for the treasure. We were going to split it fifty-fifty."

"Then I studied the design I'd copied — I remembered that hollow sound and realized the gate was filled with gold. After all this time, the pirate's treasure was right there in front of my nose," said Jackie.

"That's when you tried to break into Mr. Farrier's shop," said Henry.

"And failed," said Jackie.

"We thought the old iron fence might be made of gold, but it wasn't," added Mike.

"You found out because you came back to look. You hit the hinges with a hammer," said Violet.

Mike nodded. "We couldn't do anything else but keep an eye on you, then. Or hope I could persuade Mr. Ashleigh to convince his mother to sell us the house, gate and all."

"Forrest didn't know about this?" his mother cried out.

"No. He didn't even know who I was," said Mike. "Just that I represented somebody who would pay a lot of money for the old house."

"You kept watching us and saw Mr. Farrier deliver the gate. Then you saw us hang it up," Jessie said.

"We didn't think you knew!" said Jackie, glaring at the Boxcar Children. "I thought you'd think that this hurricane had blown it away. And we could have gotten away with it, too."

"If we hadn't set the trap," said Violet quietly.

Jackie's cheeks turned a dull, angry red.

"Ooh, that trap," she muttered.

"What do you want to do?" asked Jessie. "Should we tell the police?"

Mrs. Ashleigh looked dazed. "I don't know. I don't know what to do. But I think Jackie and Mike should leave."

The two gate thieves got up and walked to the door. Mike said to Mrs. Ashleigh, "I'm sorry. I knew it was wrong and I did it anyway. I'm sorry."

He went out.

Jackie lifted her chin. "It was pirate's gold. It was stolen in the first place. How can you steal what's already been stolen?"

She and Ellen Ashleigh stared at one another. Then Jackie said, so softly that they could barely hear her, "I'm sorry, too. That's what I get for being greedy."

She followed Mike, closing the door behind her.

And at that very moment, the lights came back on.

CHAPTER 11

The Hurricane Gate

It was time for the Aldens to go back home to Greenfield.

"It seems as if we just got here," said Violet. "Time went so fast!"

Mrs. Ashleigh patted Violet's shoulder. "Hard work and solving mysteries makes time go extra fast," she said.

"We didn't finish all the work," said Henry, looking around. "And that last big storm didn't help."

Diana, who was repairing one of the front

window shutters, said, "Don't worry. I can take care of the rest."

"We don't have to leave right this minute, do we?" asked Benny.

"No, Benny," Grandfather told him. "Not until after lunch."

"And you'll be back, Benny, won't you? For the special exhibit in the museum. The Pirate's Gate is going to be the main attraction. I expect the newspaper will even want to interview you again," said Mrs. Ashleigh.

"Okay," said Benny. He added, "Will we have our picture in the paper again, too?"

Everyone laughed.

"Maybe," said Mrs. Ashleigh.

All four Alden children, and Watch, too, had had their picture in the newspaper along with Mrs. Ashleigh. Beneath the picture was a story with the headline THE SECRET OF THE PIRATE'S GATE. Mrs. Ashleigh had donated the gate to the museum along with the papers that she and the Aldens had finally gotten organized. The story had told all about how Henry, Jessie, Violet, Benny, and Watch had figured out the secret. It had even mentioned Diana's name, because she was the one who'd first told them about the Golden Gate Bridge. And there had been a whole separate article about Mr. Farrier, since he'd known the secret, too, and since he was an expert on cast-iron and wrought-iron work.

But the story hadn't said anything about Jackie and Mike. Mrs. Ashleigh understood that Jackie was desperate for money, so she hadn't called the police. But she had warned them that if anything else at all suspicious ever happened again, she would.

They hadn't seen Jackie or Mike since then. But another, more recent article in the newspaper had been about how Hoofbeats of History was for sale because the owners were moving. Neither Jackie nor Mike's picture had been included with the article.

Again and again, Mrs. Ashleigh looked at her watch, then down the street.

"Are you expecting someone?" asked Jessie.

Just then a car pulled up out front. Forrest

Ashleigh got out. He was holding a big box.

"I thought I'd come to lunch," he said. He held up the box. "And I brought desserts. Chocolates, from a wonderful store in Charleston."

"Chocolate is my favorite thing," said Benny. He thought for a moment and said, "*One* of my favorite things."

Watch wagged his tail. Benny looked down at him. "No, Watch," he said. "Chocolate is *not* one of your favorite things. Chocolate is very bad for dogs, remember? You like dog biscuits."

Forrest came up the walk and stopped at the foot of the steps. He looked up at the Aldens and Diana and his mother. Today, he wasn't wearing a suit and tie. He was wearing jeans and an old shirt and he didn't look so much like a banker.

"But aren't you supposed to be at work, dear?" Mrs. Ashleigh said. "Shouldn't you be wearing your suit?"

"I'm taking a little time off," said Forrest. "Thinking of making some changes." He

smiled up at his mother. "I was wondering if you would let me stay here for a while. I used to have so much fun on this island when I was a kid."

"Of course. As long as you don't start talking to me about selling it," said Mrs. Ashleigh.

Forrest shook his head. "I was wrong. You have good friends and good neighbors. And you have a family. Even if a hurricane does blow this house away, it can't change that. And that's what is important."

Ellen Ashleigh nodded. "Yes," she said. "I've always known that. I'm glad you see it now, too."

Diana slapped the side of the house affectionately and they all jumped a little. They had forgotten Diana was there, working on the house. "This old house is solid as a rock," she said. "It'll take more than a hurricane to flatten it."

"Oh! I forgot to introduce you. Diana, this is my son, Forrest. Forrest, Diana Shelby. She's a carpenter — and a neighbor and friend — who's helping me fix my house," said Mrs. Ashleigh.

"A carpenter. Now, that's an interesting job," said Forrest. He went up to Diana and held out his hand. He smiled at her. She smiled back. They shook hands.

"You should buy the Hoofbeats of History tour business," said Benny loudly. "That's *really* interesting!"

Forrest turned. "Now, there's an idea," he said. "I know lots about Charleston history, since my family is part of it. I'd like to have my own business. But I'm not very handy around barns and carriages and horses."

"You could get a partner," said Violet.

Forrest looked back at Diana. "That would be a good idea," he said, smiling at her again. "A very good idea."

"Isn't it time for lunch?" asked Benny.

A horn honked. Mr. Farrier's red truck pulled up behind Forrest's car.

"Oh, good," said Mrs. Ashleigh. "That's who I was waiting for."

She went down the steps and along the

front walk to meet the blacksmith, motioning for everyone to follow.

Smiling, Mr. Farrier opened the back of his truck and lifted something out.

"The Pirate's Gate," said Jessie. "But I thought you gave it to the museum."

"No, no," said Mr. Farrier. "Wait and see."

He carried the gate to the hinges on the fence and hung it carefully in place. Then he stepped back and motioned toward it with a flourish.

"A new gate!" said Violet. "It's like the old one, but look!"

They all leaned forward to peer at the ship that was part of the design. This ship was being tossed on big waves of wrought iron beneath what looked like clouds. Beneath the ship was the figure of an old-fashioned key.

"It's a ship in a hurricane," said Henry. "But what does the key mean?"

"It means that the gate was key to the mystery. And you solved it," said Mr. Farrier.

"You did, too," said Violet.

"I *discovered* it," said Mr. Farrier. "But if you hadn't figured it out when you did, that gate might have been stolen forever."

"Did you sign it?" asked Mrs. Ashleigh.

Mr. Farrier pointed. Down near the bottom, on the back of the gate, his initials and mark were stamped into the gate, along with the date.

"It's a beautiful gate," said Mrs. Ashleigh.

"Now may we have lunch?" asked Benny.

"Of course," said Mrs. Ashleigh as everybody laughed. "Let's all go inside and have lunch and chocolates, and celebrate friends and family and mysteries solved. And the new gate — the Hurricane Mystery Gate!"

GERTRUDE CHANDLER WARNER discovered when she was teaching that many readers who like an exciting story could find no books that were both easy and fun to read. She decided to try to meet this need, and her first book, *The Boxcar Children*, quickly proved she had succeeded.

Miss Warner drew on her own experiences to write the mystery. As a child she spent hours watching trains go by on the tracks opposite her family home. She often dreamed about what it would be like to set up housekeeping in a caboose or freight car — the situation the Alden children find themselves in.

When Miss Warner received requests for more adventures involving Henry, Jessie, Violet, and Benny Alden, she began additional stories. In each, she chose a special setting and introduced unusual or eccentric characters who liked the unpredictable.

While the mystery element is central to each of Miss Warner's books, she never thought of them as strictly juvenile mysteries. She liked to stress the Aldens' independence and resourcefulness and their solid New England devotion to using up and making do. The Aldens go about most of their adventures with as little adult supervision as possible — something else that delights young readers.

Miss Warner lived in Putnam, Connecticut, until her death in 1979. During her lifetime, she received hundreds of letters from girls and boys telling her how much they liked her books.